DISNEP

5-
Minute
SNUGGLE
Stories

DISNEP PRESS

New York • Los Angeles

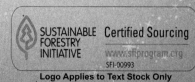

SUSTAINABLE FORESTRY INITIATIVE

Certified Sourcing

www.sfiprogram.org

SFI-00993

Logo Applies to Text Stock Only

TABLE OF CONTENTS

Thumper's Nighttime Adventure

One beautiful day, Thumper was playing outside in the sunshine. As he was exploring the forest, he spotted his friend Dizzy the opossum.

"Hiya!" Thumper said. "Want to come play?"

Dizzy yawned. "That sounds fun," he said sleepily, "but I'm getting ready for a nap. Maybe next time, okay?"

"Okay," Thumper said, and he scampered off.

Thumper and Dizzy had been friends for a while, so Thumper knew the opossum napped a lot during the day. But would Dizzy really rather sleep than play?

Later, Thumper asked his papa, "Why is Dizzy always so sleepy?"

"Ahh," said Papa. "Well, he's not *always* sleepy. Opossums are nocturnal. That means they sleep a lot during the day. Then they are awake at night, when we bunnies are sleeping."

Papa led Thumper to a nearby cave. "These bats are nocturnal, too," Papa said. "Right now, they are getting ready to rest. But they spend most of the night flying outside, looking for food."

Wow, thought Thumper. Awake all night? No wonder Dizzy was so sleepy!

That evening, as the bunnies chased fireflies,
Thumper thought about what his father had said.

Soon Dizzy will be waking up! Thumper thought. I wonder
what nocturnal animals do all night?

When Thumper and his sisters hopped home for bedtime, Thumper thought about the exciting things he might miss while he was asleep. Did the bats play tag under the stars? Did the opossum family have midnight picnics?

Before long, Thumper's sisters were sound asleep. Soon after, his mama and papa started to snore. Thumper was still wide awake.

Slowly, silently, Thumper hopped to the burrow entrance and poked his head out into the cool night breeze.

The moon was bright. The stars twinkled. Thumper went just outside the burrow and sniffed the air. He hopped a little further and sniffed again. Thumper knew he shouldn't go out without his parents' permission. But he couldn't stop thinking about the nighttime fun he was missing. . . .

Thumper's curiosity soon got the better of him, and he bounded quickly down the path.

Before Thumper knew it, he had hopped all the way to the opossums' favorite tree. Dizzy was very surprised to see Thumper. "Shouldn't you be at home, sleeping?" he asked.

Thumper giggled. "I came to see what other animals do at night," he said. "I've never been out this late before!"

"Well," Dizzy said, "my family is just about to eat breakfast. Do you want to join us?"

So Thumper had a late-night breakfast with the opossum family. They had the same blackberries Thumper usually ate during the day.

I guess nighttime breakfast isn't so different after all, Thumper thought.

After thanking the opossums, Thumper hopped away to find more nocturnal friends.

As Thumper walked through the darkness, he was startled by a voice. "Whooo's there?" Friend Owl asked from a nearby tree stump.

"It's Thumper!" the bunny replied. "Would you like to play?"

"Can't play. Looking for grass to fix up my nest!" the owl said. "Very busy night, you know."

"Can I look, too?" Thumper asked. Together, they gathered up dried grass for the inside of Friend Owl's nest. It was just like the grass on Thumper's bed!

"Thank you!" Friend Owl called as he flew away.

Thumper hopped down to the pond, where he saw some skunks. "What are you up to?" Thumper asked.

"We're off to take a bath," said one skunk.

"Some animals think that skunks stink!" said the second skunk.

"Not us!" said the third. "We take baths every night."

The skunks walked over to the shallow edge of the pond where Thumper and his sisters took their baths, too.

Thumper could take a bath anytime, so he waved to the skunks and kept on hopping.

On the far side of the pond, Thumper saw a mama duck and her ducklings snuggling together.

Thumper yawned. The ducks looked warm and comfy. And it was getting awfully late. . . .

Up in a tree, Thumper saw a squirrel and a chipmunk sound asleep. They seemed so peaceful and cozy. . . .

Hmmm, thought Thumper. They don't seem worried about missing nighttime fun.

Thumper stood very still and listened to the sounds of the night. The crickets were chirping softly. Frogs were croaking down by the river. Now and then, wings fluttered through the darkness overhead. Thumper knew they were the sounds of nighttime animals all around.

But they were also sleepy sounds.

At that moment, all Thumper wanted was to be in his burrow, snuggled up with his family.

Thumper hurried home. He hopped silently inside, expecting to find his family sleeping, just as he left them.

Instead, his sisters rushed to meet him, squeezing him from all sides.

"Oh, Thumper!" exclaimed Daisy. "We were starting to worry!"

"Thank goodness you're back!" cried Tessie.

Mama and Papa had sterner words for Thumper. "Daisy
is right. We were very worried. You could have gotten hurt,"
Papa said.

"Papa was about to go out looking for you," Mama added.

"I'm sorry," Thumper said. He hadn't meant to worry
them, but he knew he shouldn't have left without asking. "I
just . . . wondered what it's like to be nocturnal."

Papa patted Thumper's head. "I understand that you were
curious. But you must promise never, ever, ever to go out at
night without permission again."

"I promise!" Thumper said.

Thumper's parents gave him extra chores as punishment. He would have to find blackberries for dinner, gather some grass for the bunnies' beds, and take his sisters to the bathing pond.

As Thumper got ready for bed, he realized that doing chores was a little bit like his nocturnal adventure. He had eaten blackberries with the opossums, collected grass with Friend Owl, and visited with the very clean skunks.

"I guess I wasn't missing anything after all," he said to himself. Even though his nighttime adventure had been exciting, nothing was better than snuggling down in his warm, cozy burrow for a good night's sleep.

THE
LION KING

A Day Without Pumbaa

"*Mmm!*" said Timon the meerkat. "Breakfast time! Come to Daddy, you tasty little critters."

Timon was showing Simba the lion cub how to catch some very sneaky bugs in the jungle.

"Too bad Pumbaa has to miss out on this feast," Simba said as he pounced on a juicy beetle.

"I haven't seen him since sunup," Timon replied. "*Ooh!* There's a good one! Watch me, Simba—and learn!"

Timon crouched behind a rotten log crawling with beetles. He was about to pounce, when—

"AAAHHH!" Pumbaa swooped out of the trees, swinging wildly on a vine. He plowed straight into Timon, flattening the meerkat like a pancake.

"Oops! Sorry, Timon," Pumbaa said, picking himself up.

"Sorry?" shouted Timon. "*Sorry,* you say? That's the nineteenth—no, the *twentieth* time you've crashed into me this week!"

"But it wasn't on purpose," Pumbaa told him.

"You never do anything on purpose," Timon replied. "You're a *natural* disaster! Why, you couldn't catch a bug if it flew into your mouth."

"That's not true!" Pumbaa protested, tears welling up in his eyes. "Look! I'll prove it."

The clumsy warthog lunged for a juicy grub, only to fall headfirst into a puddle. Mud splattered on Simba and Timon.

"That's it!" cried Timon. "I've had it. No more disasters!"

Pumbaa looked heartbroken. "Do you think I'm a disaster, too?" he asked Simba.

"Well," Simba replied, "you have to admit, sometimes you do things that *are* pretty disastrous."

Pumbaa hung his head. "You're right," he said. "Nobody wants me around. It would be better for everyone if I just left."

With that, Pumbaa slowly plodded off into the jungle. Just then, the clouds thickened, and a bolt of lightning shot through the sky.

"Wait a second," said Simba. "Timon, we can't let him go!"

But Timon wouldn't even turn to watch his friend leave. "If that warthog thinks I'm going to beg him to stay, he's sorely mistaken," Timon said. "Trust me, Simba, he'll be back by lunchtime."

But as rain began to pour down, Simba wasn't so sure. The storm came and went. And then so did lunchtime—but still no Pumbaa. Simba began to worry.

Simba looked off in the direction Pumbaa had gone.

"We shouldn't have been so hard on him," the lion cub said. "I wonder if he's okay."

"He's fine," snapped Timon, who was still sore from getting squashed that morning. "Besides, he's the one who walked out on us, remember? *Poof!* Gone! History, as far as I'm concerned. Pumbaa? Who's that? Never heard of him!"

Simba sighed.

"Oh, stop moping," Timon continued. "And think about it. We can do anything we want now without worrying about getting knocked down, covered with mud, or run over. Let's enjoy it."

As Timon marched off, Simba followed behind.

First, Simba and Timon tried chasing vultures. Then they splashed in the river. They even tried playing a game of tag among the vines. But somehow, nothing they did seemed like very much fun. Something—or *someone*—was always missing.

"So, what do you want to do now?" Timon asked Simba.

"I don't know," replied Simba. "What do *you* want to do?"

"I asked you first," said Timon.

The sun began to dip below the horizon. Timon sighed. He was bored. And, he admitted to himself, it was also possible that he missed Pumbaa—just a little.

By the time Simba and Timon finished dinner, they werc both a little grumpy. They hadn't really enjoyed anything they'd done that day. Soon it would be bedtime, and their friend still hadn't returned.

"There's got to be something fun to do," said Simba.

"Well," Timon said gloomily, "what do *you* want to do?"

"I don't know," said Simba. "What do *you* want to do?"

The pair went on . . . and on . . . and on, trying to think of fun things to do. They would have gone on even longer, but suddenly they heard a rustling sound coming from along the riverbank.

"Timon! Simba! Look what I found!"

Wham! Pumbaa tumbled out of the jungle, knocking into Timon and Simba. Pumbaa had brought bugs for his friends, but the critters went flying into the air.

"I'm back," Pumbaa said with a groan.

"So we see," Timon mumbled from beneath the warthog.

Embarrassed, Pumbaa stood up and faced his friends. "I came back to show you all the bugs I found," he said. "But now look what I've done! I'm the worst friend ever."

"Now, wait one minute!" cried Timon. "That's just not true!"

"You're a wonderful friend, and we missed you!" Simba said. "We even missed your disasters."

Pumbaa stopped and turned toward his friends hopefully.

"It appears," Timon said with a small smile, "that we've grown accustomed to being stepped on, bruised, and squashed."

"Today was no fun without you!" Simba exclaimed. "You're our very favorite disaster."

Pumbaa rushed toward them. As he did, he accidentally knocked over Timon and stepped on Simba's paw. But this time, his friends didn't really mind.

As Simba curled up to sleep, he was already looking forward to the adventures that he would have the next day— with *both* of his friends!

Disney

Winnie the Pooh

A Good Night's Sleep

It was springtime in the Hundred-Acre Wood. Winnie the Pooh and Piglet took a walk in the warm sunshine.

"Hurray! The cold winter is over!" Piglet cheered.

"No more mittens and scarves," said Pooh.

"No more cold noses and toes," added Piglet.

"And plenty of yummy honey!" finished Pooh.

Pooh and Piglet walked until they reached
their friend Rabbit's house.

Rabbit was outside working in his garden. He
looked very tired and a little grumpy.

"What's the matter, Rabbit?" Piglet asked.
"Aren't you happy that it's spring?"

"Don't even say the word! I hate spring!" Rabbit
moaned.

Pooh and Piglet were puzzled, so Rabbit explained.
"You see that bird family up there? They sing before
the sun even comes up—right outside my bedroom
window! I can't get any sleep!"

"Oh, dear," said Piglet. "We must do something."

Pooh wasn't sure what to say to Rabbit. "Perhaps it would help if you moved somewhere else?"

Rabbit jumped up with excitement. "Oh, Pooh! What a great idea! I would love to move in with you!"

Unfortunately for Pooh, that wasn't what he meant at all! But now, it looked like he would have an unexpected guest.

So Pooh and Piglet helped move a few of Rabbit's things to Pooh's house. As they were finishing up, the bird family flew away from Rabbit's tree.

"Look!" said Pooh. "The birds are flying away!"

"They'll be back soon—singing as usual," Rabbit told him. "They're just going out to get a bite to eat."

"Oh . . ." said Pooh, a little disappointed.

When the friends reached Pooh's home, they began
unpacking.

"Rabbit," said Pooh, "you sure have brought a lot of things."

Suddenly, there seemed to be very little room for Pooh.

The next morning, Rabbit woke up early after a wonderful night of sleep.

"Rise and shine!" he called, pulling back Pooh's covers. Pooh immediately pulled them back up again. He was still sleepy!

"Pooh, it's time to get up!" scolded Rabbit. "The vegetables aren't going to plant themselves!"

Once Pooh had finally gotten out of bed, they walked to Rabbit's vegetable garden. Together, they planted seeds in neat little rows.

Perhaps bears aren't meant for such hard work, thought Pooh. But at least he could enjoy the cheerful songs of the bird family, who sang all day. Pooh rather liked their music.

Later, Piglet arrived.

"I was just over at your house, Pooh," said Piglet. "But you weren't home."

"No, I'm not home," Pooh said sadly.

Pooh took Piglet aside. "I am rather tired because Rabbit woke me up," said Pooh. "And I've got an awful rumbly in my tumbly. You see, I haven't had any honey."

Pooh wished that he could have his little house all to himself again.

"Maybe Owl will know what to do," suggested Piglet.

When Pooh and Piglet found Owl, he was too busy to help.

"I'm afraid I simply can't talk right now," Owl said. "My favorite napping branch is waiting for me." Owl flew up to an old oak tree. But a little sparrow was sitting right in Owl's favorite spot!

"It looks like my branch is already occupied!" said Owl. "I guess I'll just have to find another one!"

As Owl flew off, Pooh began to have an idea. He and Piglet hurried to Pooh's Thoughtful Spot to come up with a plan.

"We need the bird family to find a different branch to sing on," Pooh said.

"But how will we get them to move?" asked Piglet.

Pooh sat for a bit. "Think, think, think," he said as he patted his head. Finally, all of his thinking turned into a real plan.

"When the birds fly off at night to look for food, we will take their spot," said Pooh. "Then they will have to find another favorite branch."

"Just like Owl and the sparrow!" Piglet cheered.

Pooh told Rabbit about their plan to move the bird family.
Now Rabbit would be able stay in his own home without
worrying about the birds' morning songs.

"What a splendid idea," Rabbit said. "I'm glad I thought
of it!"

They moved all of Rabbit's things back into his house.

That night, Pooh and Piglet waited by the tree until the birds flew off. When they did, the friends started to climb up to the birds' favorite branch.

Rabbit offered to sit out there with them, but there was only room for two.

"At least take this blanket," said Rabbit. "And thank you for your help, dear friends."

So Pooh and Piglet waited. And waited. And waited. They tried their best so stay awake, but the blanket was awfully warm and comfortable. Soon the friends were fast asleep. The next morning, Pooh and Piglet woke up to the sound of singing birds. "Look!" Pooh said, pointing to the sky.

The bird family swooped down toward their favorite branch. But when they saw that there wasn't any room on their branch, they flew in a different direction.

"Hurray!" said Piglet. "The plan worked!"

The pair checked to see if Rabbit was asleep.

"He won't be woken up by singing birds today," said Piglet. Pooh and Piglet walked toward their homes as the sun rose over the Hundred-Acre Wood.

"I'm sure the bird family has found another favorite branch by now," said Pooh.

Pooh was right. The birds had found a new branch—right outside his window! It seemed he would have to get used to a few more unexpected guests.

Luckily, Pooh didn't mind the birds' song. He thought it sounded a bit like a lullaby. Within minutes, Pooh was once again fast asleep.

At last Rabbit, Pooh, and the bird family were all happy with their homes.

Scamp the Hero

"Be careful, Scamp!" Lady called as she watched her son dash across the yard. "Don't bounce the ball too hard."

Lady, Tramp, and their four puppies were playing together outside their home. Scamp, the only boy puppy, was just like his father—always looking for an adventure!

After they finished playing ball, Scamp asked to visit the park by himself.

"All right," Tramp told his son. "But be careful."

"I will!" promised Scamp.

Scamp bounded out past the fence and onto the sidewalk. There was so much to see beyond his yard! He stopped to watch cars that were honking and beeping at one another.

He thought about chasing them, but he remembered his promise to his father. Scamp was determined to not get into any trouble.

But it wasn't long before trouble found him! Scamp
passed an alley where a pack of big dogs were snarling at a
little white poodle. The frightened puppy was backed up
against a fence. She couldn't escape!

"Stay away from me!" the little poodle barked.

Scamp knew he had to help. He certainly couldn't fight
the other dogs, but how else could he scare them away?

Then Scamp had an idea. He carefully crept behind
a trash can and pushed it over. *CLANG! CLUNK! CRASH!*

The noise frightened the big dogs away. His trick had
worked! Unfortunately, he also made a big mess. Garbage
was everywhere.

But Scamp was more worried about the fluffy white
poodle. "Don't be frightened," he told her. "I'm friendly."

"My name is Princess," the poodle said, "and you're my hero!"

Scamp liked being someone's hero!

"Why were those dogs bothering you?" asked Scamp.

"Because they wanted this," said Princess. She pulled something out from behind a box.

"Wow!" exclaimed Scamp. It was the biggest bone he'd ever seen.

Princess offered to share the bone with Scamp. But before they could start chewing on it, two police officers walked down the alley. Scamp and Princess quickly hid.

Scamp noticed the officers pointing to the garbage can he had tipped over. Uh-oh, he thought. Scamp was worried he would be taken to the pound if they caught him. Then his parents would never let him go out on his own again.

"Let's get out of here!" Scamp whispered to Princess.

The two puppies bolted away as the policemen examined the messy alleyway.

Scamp and Princess raced down a hill and into the park. But all that running had made the puppies very thirsty! Scamp hid the bone beneath a few leaves. "Let's get a drink of water before we have this," he suggested. "It will be safe here."

But when they got back, Scamp saw that a gardener had raked the bone into a big pile of leaves!

Scamp sprang into action. He dove straight into the leaves to get the bone back.

"Hey, stop that!" yelled the gardener.

Before the gardener could catch him, Scamp grabbed the bone. He and Princess ran away once again, scattering leaves everywhere. Scamp sure was getting into a lot of trouble!

Just then, Princess spotted a stern-looking police dog. He seemed to be looking for something.

"Maybe he's looking for us because of all the trouble I've caused," Scamp worried. He thought about running away again, but Scamp remembered his promise to his parents. He knew what he had to do.

Scamp bravely stepped toward the police dog, carrying the giant bone. "What's going on here?" the police dog barked.

"I made the mess in the alley and scattered the gardener's pile of leaves," Scamp said.

But the police dog wasn't listening to Scamp. He was inspecting every inch of Princess's bone. "Yes, I think this is it," he announced.

"What?" Scamp asked.

"Let me explain," said the police dog. "Last night, there was a robbery at the museum."

"What did the thief take?" asked Scamp.

"A giant bone from our dinosaur skeleton," answered the police dog. He looked seriously at Scamp and Princess. "That bone was exactly like this one. Where did you get it?"

"I didn't steal it!" Princess exclaimed. "I found it in an alley."

"Maybe the real thief hid the bone there," suggested Scamp.

The police dog thought Scamp might be right. "Come with me," he said.

Meanwhile, Lady and Tramp were out looking for Scamp. He had been gone for a long time, and they couldn't find him anywhere.

They searched the park . . . but Scamp wasn't there!

Then they went to the pond where Scamp loved to chase the ducks . . . but Scamp wasn't there.

They even went to Tony's restaurant . . . but Scamp wasn't there, either! Lady and Tramp were starting to get very worried.

Finally, as they were walking along Main Street, they heard someone shout, "Scamp. Look over here!"

Tramp froze in his tracks. He saw a crowd of excited people at the museum down the street. The pair ran inside, hoping to find their son.

Lady and Tramp saw Scamp right away. Photographers were taking pictures of him and a white puppy!

"What's going on here?" Tramp asked Lady.

"I don't know," Lady replied, "but I'm just happy that Scamp is all right!"

When Scamp noticed his parents, he and Princess ran over to them.

"I'm sorry I didn't come straight home," Scamp told them. "But we had to help the police solve a robbery."

"Your son's a hero!" said Princess.

Tramp grinned. "That's my boy!"

"Princess was the one who found the stolen bone," Scamp said. He wasn't used to so much attention!

The director of the museum cleared his throat to make an announcement. "To thank our little heroes, we've prepared a feast." He pointed to a long table covered in treats for the puppies.

Scamp licked his lips. He had never seen so much delicious food all at once. And there were stacks of bones for him and Princess to enjoy—even if they weren't from a dinosaur!

Showtime

It didn't take long for Andy's toys to settle into their new home in Bonnie's room. Everyone had been very friendly and helpful. But many of the toys were still getting to know one another.

One morning, Dolly had an idea to help everyone become better friends. "Let's have a talent show!" she said.

"What a splendid plan!" said Mr. Pricklepants.

Soon, everyone began practicing their acts. They couldn't wait to show off their talents!

Buzz Lightyear watched his friends. They all seemed to know exactly what to do. But he wasn't sure what his act should be. He wanted it to be truly spectacular—something that would impress Jessie the cowgirl.

First, Buzz tried juggling. "Anyone need a lift?" he said to the Peas-in-a-Pod. The Peas cheered as they flew through the air.

Next, Buzz tried a karate act. "Wait till Jessie sees me do this!" he said, karate-chopping this way and that. *"Hi-ya, hi-ya, hi-ya!"*

Although his acts were both good, Buzz wasn't sure they'd impress Jessie.

Buzz looked around at the other toys. Maybe he could join one of their acts!

Buzz noticed that Mr. Pricklepants and the Little Green Aliens were practicing a play. Jessie loves to watch plays! Buzz thought as he hurried over to them.

Mr. Pricklepants greeted Buzz. "We're doing a classic: *Romeo and Juliet*!"

"Perfect!" Buzz said. "I think I'd make a great Romeo."

"Sorry, Mr. Lightyear," Mr. Pricklepants replied. "I'm afraid the only role left is Juliet's mother."

Buzz sighed. Juliet's mom wasn't exactly the role he had been hoping for.

Buzz decided to find a different group. He saw Hamm
and Buttercup working on a comedy routine. Buzz knew that
Jessie loved a good joke. If he was in their act, she would see
how funny he was!

"I can do impressions," Buzz announced as he joined his
friends. He put on a cowboy hat and said, "Howdy, partners.
I'm Sheriff Woody. Did you know that there is a snake inside
my boot?"

"I don't know about sounding like Woody," Hamm said
with a smirk. "But you definitely sound wood-*en*!"

Just then, Woody rode by on Bullseye.

"Watch how a real cowboy performs!" Woody called. He and Bullseye were great at rodeo tricks.

"What a rootin' tootin' cowboy!" Slinky said with a whistle.

Buzz had to agree. He realized that Woody made a much better cowboy than he ever could.

A few minutes later, Jessie hopped onstage, eager to get the show started.

"Are you ready to do your act, Buzz?" she asked. "I can't wait to see it."

Buzz's smile froze. "Uh-oh," he said nervously. He still hadn't decided what to do!

Bullseye turned on some music to start the show. A catchy tune filled the room.

Suddenly, Buzz's foot began twitching. Then his arm. Then his hips. The Peas rolled out of the way as Buzz kicked his legs and waved his arms.

Buzz couldn't control himself! His movements turned into dance steps—and he couldn't stop!

Buzz danced over to Jessie, spun her around, and then dipped her.

"Uh . . . I . . . I don't why I did that," Buzz apologized, blushing.

Jessie just grinned. She knew exactly what had happened: The music had switched Buzz into Spanish mode!

"It's okay, Buzz," she whispered. "Just go with it!"

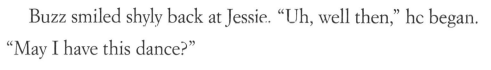

Buzz smiled shyly back at Jessie. "Uh, well then," hc began. "May I have this dance?"

Jessie nodded, and the two danced up and around the room. They dipped and twirled. They spun and whirled. And they smiled at each other the whole time.

Their friends watched, clapping and cheering for the dancing duo.

When the music ended, Buzz was beaming. He'd
finally impressed Jessie and discovered the perfect act
for the show!

"*Yee-hah!*" Jessie shouted. "What a great way to start
the show."

"That's right," agreed Buzz. "But we have one thing
left to do."

Jessie was puzzled. "What's that?"

Buzz smiled. "Take a bow!"

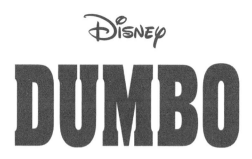

DUMBO

Dumbo's Snowy Day

Dumbo was a very special elephant—with his huge ears, he could soar through the sky like a bird. Dumbo performed in a circus with his mother, Mrs. Jumbo. One chilly day, the circus animals were on their way to a new town. But their train, Casey Jr., was struggling to get through the falling snow. His wheels slid on the icy railroad tracks.

Finally Casey Jr. decided it was too dangerous to keep going. The train came to a stop, and everyone waited for the snow to pass.

Dumbo was happy that the train had stopped. He'd
never played in the snow before! He thought it felt awfully
strange as he tried to walk through it. The snow pressed
against his feet like cold sand.

"You can do it!" said Mrs. Jumbo. She gave him a gentle
nuzzle.

Soon Dumbo got the hang of walking through the snow.
He liked the *crunch-crunch-crunch* sound he heard with
every step.

All morning, Dumbo and his mother played in the snow. They gathered snowballs together with their trunks. They made snow elephants. They even played hide-and-seek! But as Dumbo and his mother explored, they got farther and farther away from the waiting train.

Suddenly, Dumbo slid down a steep hill. He called after his mother to follow him. But when she reached the bottom of the hill, Mrs. Jumbo realized she couldn't climb back up!

Dumbo tried to push. He tried to pull. But nothing worked. Mrs. Jumbo slipped farther down the slope toward a sharp cliff edge.

"You will have to fly off and get help," Mrs. Jumbo told him.

So off Dumbo flew, as fast as his ears would take him. As he soared toward the train, the wind began to blow. It pushed harder and harder against him. The snow stung his eyes, and the cold nipped at his toes.

Finally, Dumbo's ears got so cold he couldn't fly. As he waited for the wind to pass, he worried about his mother.

Once the wind died down, Dumbo raced back to the train. Quickly, he gathered all the animals together so that they could help.

"What are we waiting for?" Timothy Mouse cried. "We've got to save Mrs. Jumbo!"

Dumbo led his friends back to the cliff.

By the time they found Mrs. Jumbo, the windstorm had pushed her even closer to the cliff's edge. The animals knew they had to think of something fast!

"Oh, dear," worried the giraffe. "How can we get down there to help?"

Timothy snapped his fingers—he had an idea.
"Everybody line up!" he shouted. He ordered the
animals to grab one another's tails. At the front of the
line, the ostrich leaned over the cliff to take hold of
Mrs. Jumbo's trunk.

"One, two, three, PULL!" Timothy yelled.

The animals worked together, huffing and puffing, pulling and stretching, until Mrs. Jumbo made it safely to the top of the cliff.

"Hooray!" everyone shouted.

Suddenly, there was a loud *CRACK!*

The cliff side gave way, and the animals tumbled down.

"Watch out!" yelled the hippo.

"Yikes!" cried the monkeys.

"Uh-oh!" said the giraffe.

"Help!" hollered the bear.

All of the animals tumbled together and rolled down the
hill. Before long, they had become a giant snowball!

"How do you stop this thing?" Timothy shouted as they
zoomed along.

The snowball gathered speed until . . .

Crash! Bang! Boom! Oof!

The animal snowball hit the bottom of the hill and broke apart!

"Is everyone okay?" Timothy asked as he straightened his hat.

Luckily, everyone was fine—just a little dizzy from their unexpected snow ride. All the animals began walking back to the train. Walking wasn't nearly as fast as riding a snowball, but it was a lot less scary!

That night, Mrs. Jumbo gave Dumbo a warm bath.

"Thank you for flying to find help today," Mrs. Jumbo said to her son. "I'm so proud of you."

Dumbo smiled and blew a trunk full of water over his head.

"Hey! Don't forget about me," said Timothy from his teacup bath. "I helped, too!"

Mrs. Jumbo nodded. "You certainly did. Thank you."

"Aw, gee," said Timothy. "It was nothing. Nothing at all."

Then it was time for bed. Dumbo snuggled up against his mother, and Timothy nestled underneath Dumbo's ear. "Good night, my darling," Mrs. Jumbo said softly.

"Sleep tight!" said Timothy.

Dumbo fell asleep right away. Tomorrow he and the circus animals would perform for hundreds of happy children in the new town. But for now, Dumbo was glad to be warm and safe with his mother as the snow fell gently outside.

Bambi

The Winter Trail

One winter morning, Bambi was sleeping softly when he heard a thumping sound nearby.

"Come on, Bambi!" his bunny friend, Thumper, called. "It's a perfect day for playing."

Bambi got up and followed Thumper through the forest. It was a beautiful day! The sky was blue and sunny, and the ground was covered in a blanket of new snow. Icicles glistened on the trees as Bambi and Thumper raced beneath the frozen branches.

As the two friends played, they came across a line of footprints in the snow. "Look at these tracks!" Thumper said excitedly. "Who do you suppose they belong to?"

The friends decided to follow the footprints, hoping to meet the animal who had left the trail.

Before long, they came to a tree and saw someone who
might have made the snowy tracks.

"Wake up, Friend Owl!" called Thumper.

The bird peered down at the animals. He had only just
flown to his favorite tree branch and fallen asleep. "Stop
that racket!" he replied crossly, and closed his eyes.

Bambi and Thumper giggled. Friend Owl was always
grouchy when they woke him up.

"Friend Owl, have you been out walking?" Bambi asked.

"Now why would I do that?" Friend Owl replied, opening
his eyes. "My wings take me everywhere I need to go."

"Oh, I see," Thumper said. "Thanks anyway!"

So the two friends continued to follow the snowy
footprints.

Soon Bambi and Thumper met up with their friend
Faline. "You can help us find whoever made these tracks,"
said Bambi, pointing to the trail.

Faline nodded and began to walk with them.

"We should see if Flower wants to come, too," Faline
said. Flower was their skunk friend.

But when they found Flower, he was fast asleep.

Thumper tried to wake Flower, but the little skunk just mumbled, "See you next spring," without even opening his eyes.

The three friends decided to keep going without him.

Thumper bounded down the path. He followed the footprints to a frozen pond and glided across. "Come on!" he called. "There are tracks over here, too."

So Faline and Bambi started to cross the pond. Before long, Faline had joined Thumper on the other side. But Bambi wasn't a very good skater. His hooves slipped backward and forward until he fell flat on the ice!

"Aw, Bambi," Thumper giggled. "It's okay. We can go
skating later, and I'll even show you how to spin around."

After a lot of slipping and sliding, Bambi finally took a
running start and sped across the pond on his belly.

"You made it!" Faline cheered.

Next the three friends walked up a snowy hill. At the top, they spotted a raccoon sitting by a tree trunk, eating some berries.

"Hello, Mr. Raccoon," Faline said. "Did you happen to see who made these tracks in the snow?"

But the raccoon's mouth was so full he couldn't say anything! He shook his head and began tapping the tree.

The friends looked around. Then they heard a *tap-tap-tap* in the distance.

"I know!" Thumper cried. "He thinks we should ask the woodpeckers."

"Oh, thank you," Bambi said. The raccoon waved good-bye as the friends headed down the path toward the woodpeckers' pine grove.

The tapping got louder and louder. Soon Bambi, Faline,
and Thumper had found the woodpeckers. The mama was
pecking away, and her three children were sitting in holes in
the tree trunk. They stuck their heads out when they heard
Thumper call, "Helloooooooo!"

"Yes?" the mama bird replied.

"Did you make the tracks in the snow?" Thumper asked.

"No, we've been here all day," she answered.

"Yes, yes, yes," her babies added.

Just then, Faline noticed that the trail continued behind
the tree.

Bambi and Thumper chatted excitedly as they walked. "If the tracks don't belong to the woodpeckers, and they don't belong to the raccoon, and they don't belong to Friend Owl, whose can they be?" Bambi asked.

Suddenly, Thumper stopped and looked down. They had finally reached the end of the trail! The tracks led all the way to a snowy bush, where a family of quail was resting.

"Did you make these tracks?" Thumper asked Mrs. Quail.

"Why, yes," she answered. "Friend Owl told me about this wonderful bush. So this morning, my babies and I walked all the way over here."

Thumper, Bambi, and Faline cheered. They had
solved the mystery of the strange tracks—and they had
spent a beautiful day visiting friends.

"Oh dear," Faline said as she saw the sun setting over
the hill. "I think it's time for us to go home."

But when they turned to leave, a big surprise was waiting for them—their mothers!

Thumper was confused. "How did you find us?" he asked.

Thumper's mama answered, "Well, your sisters pointed us in the right direction and then . . ." She looked down at the deer and rabbit tracks that the three friends had left in the snow.

"You followed our trail!" Faline cried. Her mother nodded.

"Now, let's follow it back home," Bambi's mother said.

And that's just what they did.

DISNEY·PIXAR
MONSTERS, INC.

What I Did on My Summer Vacation

Mike Wazowski raced toward the giant front doors of Monsters, Inc. He wanted to get to work early because he was collecting laughs from his friend Boo.

"Hey, kiddo!" Mike said when he got to Boo's bedroom.

He immediately began telling jokes and acting silly. Boo was happy to see the one-eyed monster, but she didn't laugh quite as much as usual.

"Is something wrong?" Mike asked.

Boo pointed to some hand-drawn pictures on her wall. There was one of her school and another of kids holding up photos. Mike wasn't quite sure what Boo was trying to tell him. "You . . . need pictures of a school?" Mike guessed.

Boo shook her head and pointed to herself, then to a drawing of a camera.

Mike was still confused. "You want to go to photography school?"

Boo laughed and shook her head again.

Finally, after a lot of pointing and drawing, Mike figured out what Boo was trying to tell him. School began the next day, and she didn't have any summer vacation pictures to show her class.

"Why don't you come to Monsters, Inc. with me?" Mike suggested. "I have a camera you can borrow. And we can surprise Sulley!"

Boo and Mike stepped through Boo's closet door and into Monsters, Inc. It was very unusual for a child to travel to the monster world. But Mike didn't think anyone would mind. After all, Boo had been to Monsters, Inc. before.

It was still early, so there weren't any monsters on the Laugh Floor yet.

"Follow me," said Mike. "The camera should be right over here."

Mike took Boo to a supply closet and grabbed his old camera. "Let's see if it still works," he said.

As Boo tried to take a picture, the camera's bright flash went off. *"AHHH!"* cried Mike.

Boo laughed so hard that the lights flickered.

"Yup, I guess it works." Mike smiled and rubbed his sore eye.

Then Mike led Boo back to the Laugh Floor. It was now full of monsters getting ready for work. "Oh, Sulleeey!" he called out to his friend. "I have a surprise for you."

"Kitty!" Boo exclaimed, using her nickname for her furry friend. Sulley was so happy to see her. He wrapped her in a big hug.

Everyone on the Laugh Floor was excited to see
Boo. Many of the monsters showed off their new
tricks. Boo made sure to take pictures of everyone!

Next, Mike and Sulley took Boo to the beach, then to an amusement park. They went all over Monstropolis trying to pack a whole summer's worth of fun into just a few hours!

By the end of the visit, Boo had lots of photos. She and
Mike tried to decide which pictures were the best ones to
take to school.

But when Sulley heard what they were planning,
he frowned.

"You know that's against the rules!" Sulley told Mike.

"Gee, Sulley. I was just trying to help," Mike said.

Sulley sighed. "I know, Mikey, but it's my job to
protect Monsters, Inc. We have to keep the monster
world a secret from the human world."

"How are we going to tell Boo?" asked Mike.

Sulley looked over his shoulder. Boo was already
looking sad.

Sulley hated to see Boo so disappointed.

"Please, Kitty?" she said.

"Okay," Sulley said finally. "I'll let you take back one photo. But I get to pick which one."

Boo cheered.

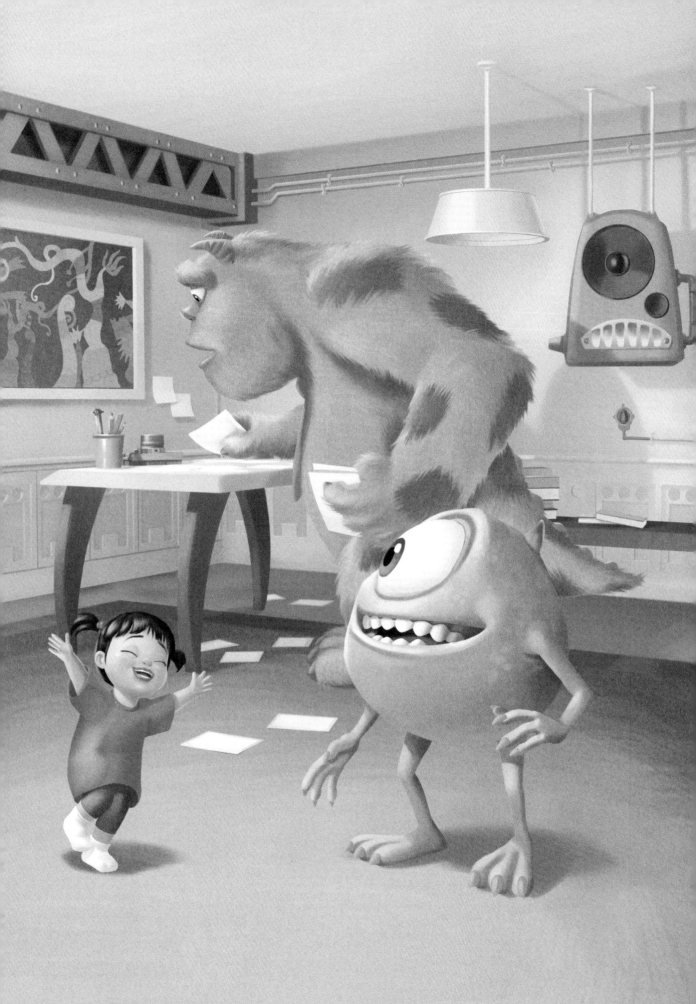

At school the next day, Boo told her class all
about her special adventure.

Her classmates didn't believe her.

Her teacher didn't believe her.

So Boo pulled out the picture. . . .

The teacher gasped. "That looks like Bigfoot!"

"No." Boo giggled. "Kitty!"

Because the photo was so blurry, none of her classmates believed her story. But Boo didn't care. With Mike, Sulley, and all her monster friends, she'd had the best summer vacation ever!

MINNIE MOUSE

Scaredy-cat Sleepover

Minnie Mouse rolled her pretty pink suitcase up to her best friend Daisy Duck's front door. She and Daisy were having a sleepover! The door flew open before Minnie even had a chance to ring the bell.

"Hurry up!" cried Daisy. "I've got a ton of stuff planned for us to do!"

When they got inside, Daisy announced, "First, we're making cupcakes!" The friends got right to work mixing, baking, and decorating.

"These look amazing, if I do say so myself," Daisy said.

"Tomorrow, let's leave some at Mickey's and
Donald's houses as a surprise," Minnie suggested. Then
she noticed the cupcakes were decorated just like the
bows they were wearing. "Somehow I have a feeling
they'll know the cupcakes are from us!"

Next it was time for a fashion show. Daisy brought out makeup, jewelry, and some of her most glamorous clothes.

"We are going to look so cute!" Daisy said.

When they were done, Minnie looked at herself in the mirror. "I'm not so sure about cute," she said, laughing. "I think I accidentally made myself into a Christmas tree!"

Minnie decided that "Christmas Tree" was probably not the next big fashion trend. So she and Daisy ditched their new looks and changed into pajamas. It was time to relax and enjoy a movie.

"My TV gets three hundred ninety-seven channels," said Daisy. "Let's see what looks good!"

They channel-surfed until they came to a scary-movie marathon.

"Perfect!" Minnie said.

A movie called *The Invisible Monster with Ten-Foot Claws* was just beginning. Minnie and Daisy watched as an actress entered a spooky mansion. The door slammed behind her with a *BANG!*

"*Eeek!*" Minnie and Daisy jumped.

"You'll never get me, monster!" the actress cried. But soon she heard the *scratch, scratch, scratch* of the monster moving toward her.

The monster chased the actress all over the house.

Luckily, she managed to escape. But Minnie and Daisy watched the rest of the movie with the lights on.

When the movie was over, the friends got ready for bed.
Minnie tried not to jump every time she heard a strange
sound. Daisy tried to ignore the creepy shadows on the wall.
Soon, they got into bed and wished each other sweet dreams.

But an hour later, they were still awake.

"That movie scared me," Minnie finally admitted. "Somehow
an invisible monster is even worse than one you can see. Just
imagining what it might look like gave me goose bumps!"

"I got goose bumps, too," replied Daisy. She tried to cheer
up her friend by making a joke. "Especially when that girl wore
the ugly sweater with mustard-yellow sparkles. I've never seen
anything so frightening!"

Minnie suggested they drink some warm milk to make themselves sleepy. After two big mugs full, they were back in bed . . . and still awake.

"It's not working," Daisy groaned. "What should we do now?"

"How about counting sheep?" Minnie replied. She closed her eyes and began picturing a meadow full of them.

Daisy closed her eyes too, but she decided to count other things instead.

Finally, the girls started to drift off. Then, suddenly, they heard a loud *SCRATCH*!

"What was that?" Daisy cried.

"I don't know," Minnie said, huddling under her blanket. "Maybe it was just a branch scraping against the window?"

"Yes, that must be it," replied Daisy, but she wasn't convinced.

A few minutes later, they heard more scratching, and
then a loud *SCREECH!*

"Aaaahhh!" yelled the girls.

"What if it's the Invisible Monster with Ten-Foot Claws?"
asked Daisy.

Minnie took a deep breath. "Let's try to stay calm," she
said. "I'm sure whatever is making those noises is perfectly
harmless—and there's only one way to find out."

"What's that?" asked Daisy.

"We have to be like the girl in the movie and investigate," said Minnie.

"Okay." Daisy nodded nervously. "But I'm not dressing like her!"

So the pair tiptoed toward the sound of the scratching.
It seemed to be coming from outside the front door.

"Let's peek out the window," suggested Daisy. "Maybe we
can see something."

Minnie pulled aside the curtain and let out a loud gasp.

"What is it?" asked Daisy.

"Kittens!" cried Minnie.

She quickly threw open the door and brought them inside.

"Poor things. Do you think they're lost?" Daisy asked.

"Maybe," Minnie replied. "We'll ask around the neighborhood tomorrow and see if they belong to anyone."

"In the meantime, I'll make up the spare bed," said Daisy.

"What spare bed?" Minnie wondered.

Daisy grabbed her laundry basket. "This one!" she said.

"Who would have guessed that our monster would turn out to be furry and cute?" Minnie asked as she snuggled back into her sleeping bag.

"Not me!" Daisy replied, and the two girls burst into giggles.

Just a few minutes later, Minnie, Daisy, and the not-so-scary kittens were all fast asleep!

Disney Princess
Tangled

Rapunzel's Forest Friends

Rapunzel was having an amazing day. It all started when she met a new friend named Flynn. With him as her guide, she had left the tower she lived in for the first time ever! Now she was running barefoot through the forest, feeling the sun on her face and the soft grass beneath her feet.

Everything around her was a discovery—from the tallest tree to the tiniest pebble. Rapunzel wanted to learn about all of it! She stopped to smell some flowers and picked a few more to add to her bouquet.

"These are so beautiful!" she exclaimed. "What are they called—*AAAAAAH!*"

A branch in the bushes had started to move-—only it wasn't a branch. It was a pair of antlers. And the animal with the antlers was now staring at Rapunzel! She stumbled backward, tripped over her flowing hair, and fell down.

Rapunzel scrambled to her feet and hid behind Flynn.
"It's just a deer," he said. Then a smaller creature with long
ears hopped out of the bushes. "What is that?!" she cried.

"Hey, whoa, easy," Flynn said. "Okay, I can see you
haven't been introduced. Rapunzel, meet the fiercest
animal in the forest: a wittle bunny-wabbit."

A whole family of bunnies hopped out of the bushes
and began playing together. Rapunzel peeked at them
from behind Flynn.

"You're telling me that a tough cookie like you is
afraid of a couple of fuzzballs?" Flynn asked over his
shoulder.

Rapunzel didn't want Flynn to think she was afraid. So
she slowly made her way closer to the bunnies and knelt
down on the grass. They seemed just as curious about her
as she was about them. Soon she was surrounded by new
furry friends.

A chipmunk scurried out of his hole and birds flew over to join the little group. Before long, Rapunzel and the animals were playing a game of hide-and-seek.

"This is the most fun I've had in . . . forever!" she told them. Rapunzel had only been out of her tower a short while, and she was already having the time of her life!

But someone else wasn't having any fun. Flynn
tapped his foot impatiently. "So if playtime is just
about over," he said, "maybe we could move on? Mosey
along? Get going? What do you say?"

"Come on!" Rapunzel called to Flynn. "Don't just stand there. Go hide! It's my turn to count."

Flynn laughed at the idea. "Uh, no. I don't do games," he said.

The animals wanted Flynn to play, too. The birds
and the chipmunk brought over some leaves and twigs
to help him get started on a hiding place.

"Hey! Quit it!" Flynn cried, shooing them away.

Then the bunnies and the deer tried to help. If Flynn
wasn't going to build a hiding place, maybe they could build
one *for* him.

But the animals had trouble covering him completely!
And there was definitely no hiding the scowl on Flynn's face.

"Never mind," Rapunzel said to her friends. "I guess he really doesn't want to play." And with that, she led the animals away for another round of games.

Rapunzel called back to Flynn, "If you change your mind, we'll be over here, having a wonderful time!"

But Rapunzel didn't stay away for long.

Minutes later, she hurried back to show Flynn the new animal she'd found.

"Oh, my goodness!" Rapunzel cried as she burst out of the bushes. "Look at this cute guy. I had no idea bunnies could grow so big!"

"That's no bunny!" shouted Flynn.

"Then what is he?" Rapunzel asked.

"BEAR!" Flynn yelled. Then he spotted the bear cub's mama. "I mean, TWO BEARS!"

153

In a panic, Flynn turned and scrambled up a tree. Rapunzel watched from below with her two new friends. She didn't understand how Flynn could be afraid of such adorable animals.

"Oh, great! *Now* you're hiding!" Rapunzel teased. "I guess you do want to play with us after all!"

155

Flynn sighed. If Rapunzel could get over her fear of bunnies, maybe he could be friends with a bear. He turned his back to Rapunzel and started climbing down the tree. "All right, fine. I'll play," he said as his feet hit the ground. "You'll see, I'm excellent at hiding."

He turned. Rapunzel was gone. So were the animals.

"I'm sure you are," came Rapunzel's voice from the bushes. "But you'll have to find us first!"

The Birthday Wish

"Good night, my loves," Duchess said. Her tail swished softly as she gave each of her kittens—Berlioz, Toulouse, and Marie—a tender nuzzle.

"Sleep tight, kiddos," O'Malley said as he tucked them in.

Berlioz and Toulouse purred happily, but Marie didn't want to go to bed. "*Please* may I go to the party tonight?" she asked. "I promise to be very good!"

Duchess smiled and shook her head. "Scat Cat will have other birthday parties you can go to when you're older. For now, you need a good night's sleep."

Duchess and O'Malley left and shut the door quietly behind them.

Marie listened as Berlioz began to snore softly. Then Toulouse's whiskers began twitching. Soon both her brothers were fast asleep.

But Marie was wide awake.

Voices drifted from downstairs, then music. Duchess and
O'Malley were throwing a birthday party for their friend Scat Cat.
He was a jazz musician who had helped Duchess and the kittens
when they were separated from their owner.

Marie sighed. Oh, how she wished she were allowed to join
them! Why, Scat Cat was her friend, too. It wasn't fair! After all,
Marie could laugh and dance and sing as well as any grown-up.

That's it! Marie thought. She could sneak into the party if she looked like an adult. Tiptoeing carefully, she made her way down the stairs. The coat closet would be full of things she could use to disguise herself!

The noise from the ballroom became louder as Marie slipped into the dark closet. She rummaged around, trying things on. The feather boa tickled her nose. The frilly bonnet wasn't glamorous enough for a party. The dark glasses made it impossible for Marie to see anything. Finally, she found the perfect disguise. Marie thought she looked very grown-up.

Marie crept into the parlor and looked around. Scat Cat was leading the band in a fast-paced jazz number. Duchess and O'Malley were chatting with some cats in the corner. But most of the cats were dancing. They danced on the floor, on tables— there was even a cat swinging from the chandelier!

Marie wanted to dance, too. "But I have to stay quiet," she reminded herself. "I mustn't get caught!"

"This is a beautiful house," someone said. Marie turned around to see a lady cat wearing a sparkly collar. She was talking to Marie!

"Thank you," Marie said. Then she slapped a paw over her mouth. She was in disguise as a guest. No one could know this was her house!

"I mean," Marie added in a hurry, "I think so, too."

The lady cat gave Marie a funny look. Marie decided to change the subject, fast.

"I like your collar," she said.

"I like your hat," the cat said. Marie beamed. It was working! Her disguise was *perfect*.

Nearby, a cat in an apron appeared, carrying a large platter. "Who wants tuna ice cream?" he said.

"I do! I do!" Marie raised her hand and jumped up and down. Then she remembered—she was supposed to act like a grown-up tonight!

The aproned cat handed her a bowl. "Thank you very much, young fellow," Marie said in her best adult voice. As she tasted the ice cream, she purred loudly. Tuna was her favorite!

Later, some of the guests played party games. Marie enjoyed the charades, but Pin the Tail on the Doggie was her favorite. She won every round!

As Marie removed her blindfold, the band started playing a
new tune. Scat Cat put his trumpet down.

"You're on your own, fellas!" he said to the band. "This
birthday cat has got a date with the dance floor." Scat Cat
walked over to Marie. "Ma'am," he said with a wink, "may I
have this dance?"

Marie forgot all about getting in trouble. She put her little paw in his, and Scat Cat led her out onto the dance floor.

"Enjoying the party, Marie?" Scat Cat asked.

"Oh, yes!" Marie replied. Then she gasped. "I mean . . . who's Marie?" she asked, trying to cover up her mistake.

"Don't worry. Your secret is safe with me," Scat Cat said. "Let's just dance!"

The music swelled, and Marie took Scat Cat's advice. She swayed, bopped, and jumped to the beat. Then, as the piano trilled, Scat Cat spun her around like a top. Marie whirled— and her disguise went flying off!

"Marie!"

The music stopped, and everyone stared. Marie's disguise was gone, and her mother was marching right toward her!

"Young lady, you are supposed to be in bed!" Duchess said.

Marie looked up sadly. "I'm sorry, Mama," she said. "I didn't mean to disappoint you." Marie felt terrible for making her mother angry.

"Hey now," said a rumbly voice. Marie looked up. It was Scat Cat!

"Say, Duchess, it *is* my birthday," Scat Cat said, "and Marie's my friend. How about letting her stay?" Scat Cat leaned over toward the birthday cake on the table. "It's my birthday wish!" he said. Then he blew out all the candles and winked at Marie. She smiled back.

Duchess sighed, looking closely at Marie and Scat Cat. "Well, just this once, I suppose. But you are going to bed early tomorrow night, Marie. Understood?"

Marie nodded happily. "Thank you, Mama! I promise I'll never sneak out again."

So Marie stayed at the party, singing and dancing and talking with the grown-ups. Finally, it was time for everyone to go home. Marie was as sleepy as she had ever been. As Duchess carried her up to bed, Marie heard Scat Cat call, "Thanks for coming to my party, Marie!"

"Happy birthday, Scat Cat!" Marie called back. "Thank you for the dance!"

Marie couldn't stop smiling as Duchess tucked her back into bed with her brothers. She would never forget her special night and Scat Cat's birthday wish!

DONALD DUCK

Donald's Building Disaster

One afternoon, Donald Duck was outside working in his garden. Suddenly, he heard the loud rumble of a truck coming from next door.

"What a racket!" he grumbled to himself. Donald walked over to the fence and asked his neighbor what was going on.

"These workers are setting up my brand-new shed!" the neighbor exclaimed. "Isn't it fabulous?"

Donald's neighbor was always bragging about the things he owned.

Donald looked at his own broken-down shed and felt jealous. But then he had an idea. "Wait until you see my new shed."

Donald didn't have enough money to buy a new shed. But that didn't stop him.

"I'll just knock down the old shed and build a new one," he declared. "And it will be *much* better than my pesky neighbor's!"

He changed his clothes, grabbed his tools, and got to work.

Donald had no idea that two little chipmunks named Chip and Dale lived inside the shed. When Donald began pulling apart the old boards, the noise woke them up.

"Oh, no!" cried Dale as he peeked outside. "That duck is tearing down our home!"

"What can we do?" wondered Dale.

The hammering grew louder and louder as the chipmunks tried to think of a plan.

"I know!" said Chip. "We'll break his hammer so he can't get any work done."

The chipmunks waited for Donald to take a rest. Then they scurried to his toolbox and pulled out the hammer. Chip and Dale gnawed on the handle until it was almost in two pieces.

When they were done, they ran back inside the shed to watch what would happen.

Soon Donald returned to finish tearing down the shed. He picked up the hammer and started prying a nail from one of the wooden planks. Suddenly, the hammer broke in half! The heavy metal top fell right off—and onto Donald's foot!

"*Ow!!!*" Donald wailed, jumping around. He hobbled into the house to find a bandage.

"Our home is saved!" cheered Chip and Dale.

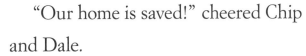

But Donald wasn't ready to give up! "I'll show that crazy neighbor of mine whose shed is the best!" he said, limping back outside.

If he couldn't use his hammer, Donald would just need to find a new tool. He rummaged through his toolbox until he found a crowbar. "This should do it!"

Inside, the chipmunks began to worry.
Board by board, their home was being destroyed!
"I don't know if we can stop him," Dale said. "We might
have to find a new home!"

"No way!" insisted Chip. "We just need a new plan."

"Maybe we can use something in the shed to frighten
him away?" Dale suggested.

While Chip kept a lookout, Dale searched for the scariest thing he could find.

"How about this?" Dale said, holding up a spool of thread.

Chip laughed. "That's not scary! We need somcthing bigger."

"I've got it!" Chip exclaimed. "Let's
use the lawn mower to chase him away!"

Chip climbed onto the mower and
pulled the starter cord as hard as he could.
The machine rumbled to life with a loud
VROOM! But it just sat there.

"Maybe you need to give it a push?" Dale suggested.

Chip gently pushed against the side of the lawn
mower. It moved inch by inch until, suddenly, it
zoomed out the door . . .

. . . right toward Donald!

"Help!" Donald yelled, fleeing from the runaway lawn mower. Plants, flowers, and grass were all mowed down as the machine zigzagged across the garden.

Donald ran behind the shed, trying to hide from the crazy machine. But the mower smashed right into the wobbly building. It shook . . . and creaked . . . and finally fell apart!

When the dust settled, all that was left of the shed was a pile of planks, with two confused chipmunks on top.

"Our plan didn't work at all!" moaned Dale. "The lawn mower wasn't supposed to come back!"

When Donald spotted Chip and Dale, he quickly figured out what had happened.

"I'll get you for this!" Donald yelled as the two chipmunks skittered up a tree. Donald stayed by the tree all afternoon, trying everything he could to get the chipmunks to come down.

He was still there when his nephews, Huey, Dewey, and Louie, came home from school.

"What are you doing, Uncle Donald?" Huey asked.

"Those no-good pests were trying to stop me from tearing down my shed," Donald explained. "But I beat them in the end . . . if I could just get them down from there!"

The boys didn't think Chip and Dale looked like "no-good pests." In fact, they thought the chipmunks were pretty cute. The three brothers put their heads together to come up with a plan.

"Uncle Donald, remember how you promised us that we could get a pet?" asked Huey.

"We could keep the chipmunks," explained Dewey.

"And we promise they won't cause any more trouble!" finished Louie.

"Hmmmm . . ." Donald thought about their idea. "But where would the chipmunks live?"

"We can use the wood from the old shed to build them a new house!" Dewey said.

"A chipmunk house?" Donald asked. "My neighbor definitely doesn't have one of those. . . ."

So Donald agreed, and the boys got to work. Before long, Chip and Dale had a beautiful new home.

Donald couldn't wait to tell his neighbor about the new chipmunk house. "The boys built it themselves!" he said excitedly.

"Oh, a chipmunk house. I had one of those put in last week," the neighbor replied. "It has four stories and a swimming pool."

Donald couldn't believe his neighbor had still outdone him! But the boys didn't care, and neither did Chip and Dale. They were all too busy playing with their new friends. And as Donald watched them having fun, he realized that everything might have turned out all right after all.